This book
belongs to:

....

This paperback first published in 2014 by Andersen Press Ltd.
First published in Great Britain in 2014 by Andersen Press Ltd., 20 Vauxhall Bridge Road, London SW1V 2SA.
Published in Australia by Random House Australia Pty., Level 3, 100 Pacific Highway, North Sydney, NSW 2060.

Copyright © Bob Staake, 2013.
Published by arrangement with Random House Children's Books, a division of Random House LLC, New York, USA.
The rights of Bob Staake to be identified as the author and illustrator of this work have been asserted
by him in accordance with the Copyright, Designs and Patents Act, 1988.
All rights reserved. Colour separated in Switzerland by Photolitho AG, Zürich.
Printed and bound in Singapore by Tien Wah Press.

10   9   8   7   6   5   4   3   2   1

British Library Cataloguing in Publication Data available.

ISBN 978 1 78344 185 3

To John James Audubon

Welcome, Class
Mrs. Albert
Room 12

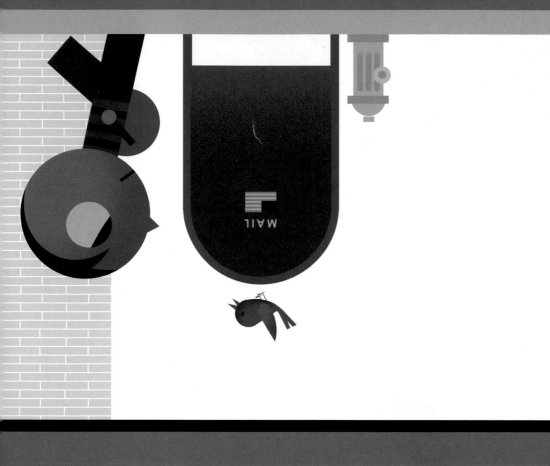
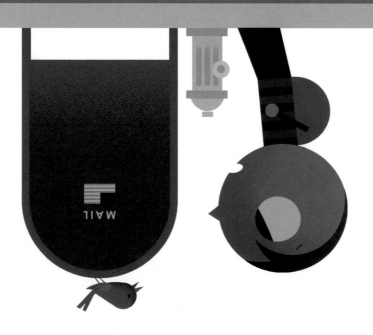

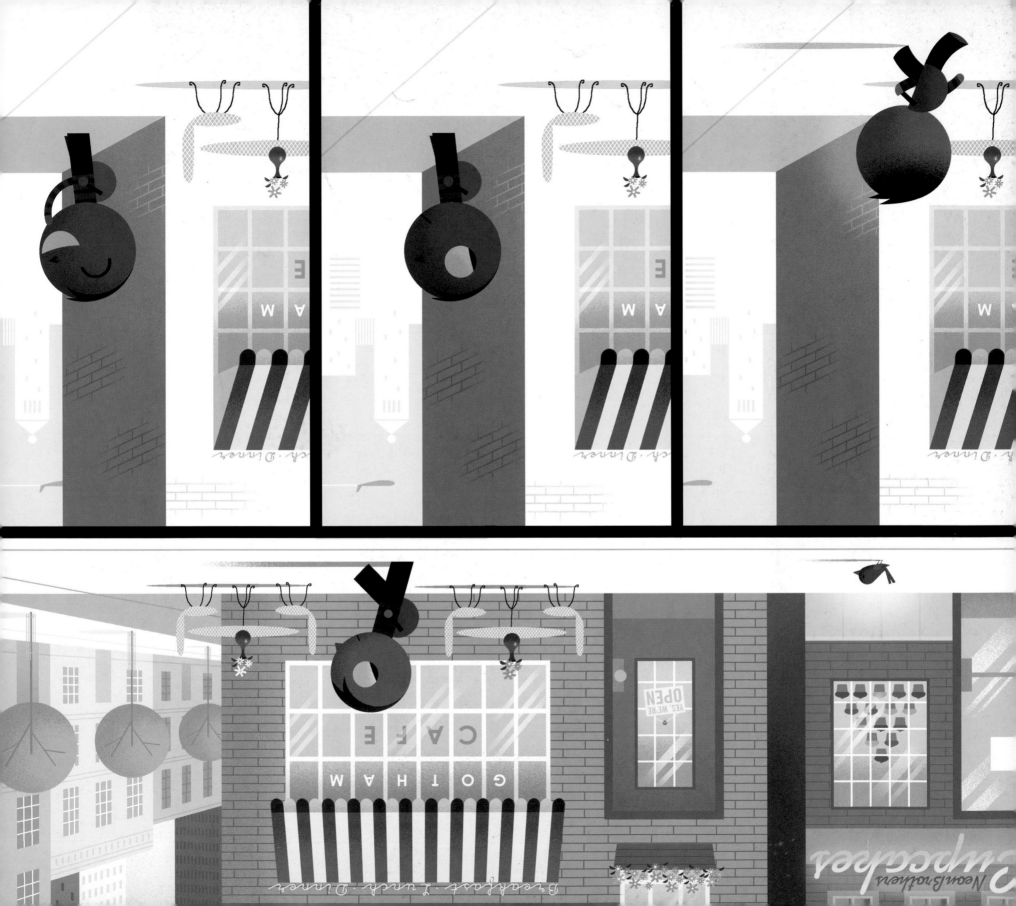

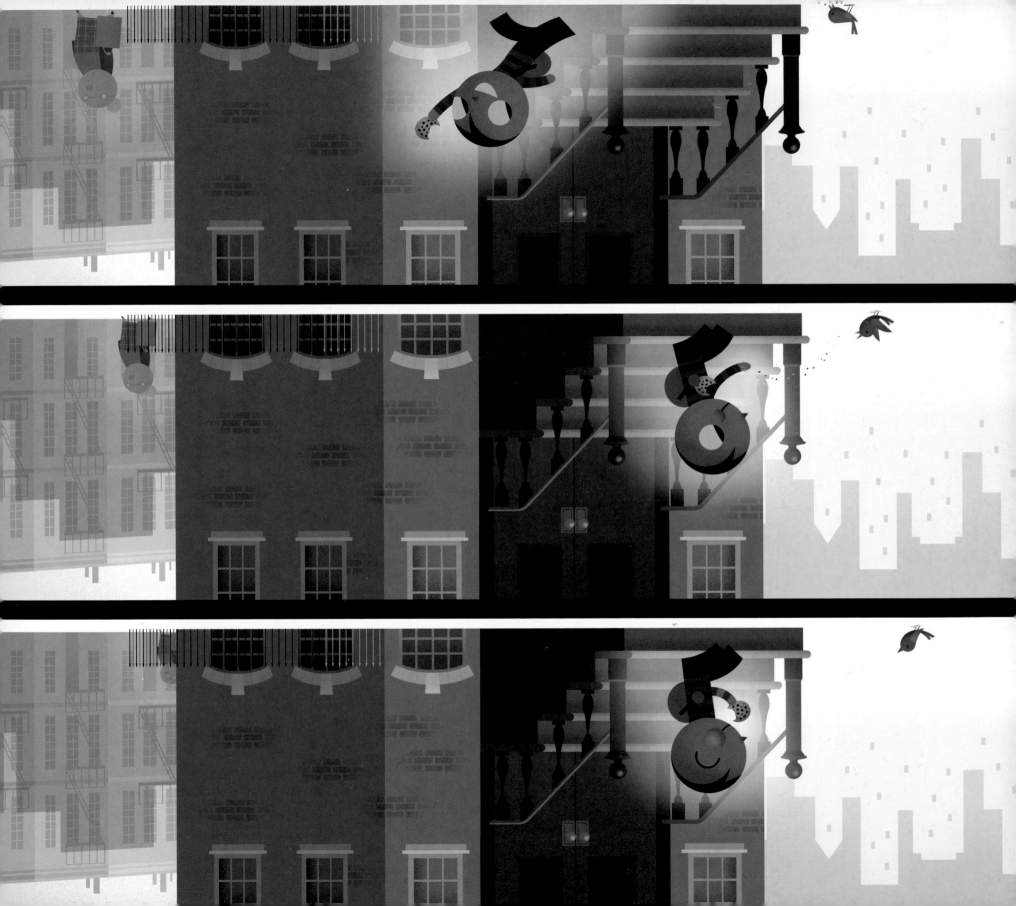

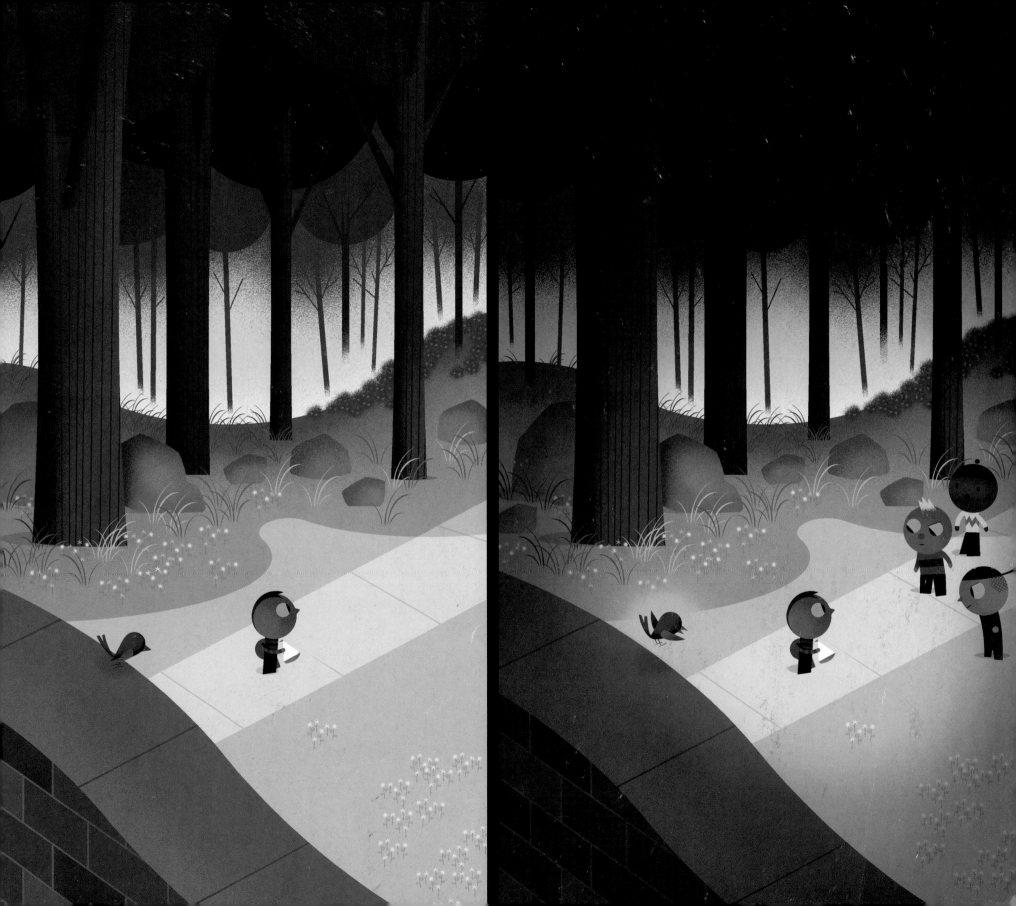